Welcome, Precious

Welcome, Precious

NIKKI GRIMES

ILLUSTRATIONS BY

BRYAN COLLIER

ORCHARD BOOKS · NEW YORK

AN IMPRINT OF SCHOLASTIC INC.

Welcome, Precious.

Welcome to a world

wrapped in rainbow.

Welcome to robin song

and the swish of leaves in the breeze.

Welcome to the silk of grass,
the satin of rose petals,
and the squish of sand
between your toes.

Welcome to rain-swept earth
and spiced cider on the wind.

Welcome to sun-sparkle
and moonlight.

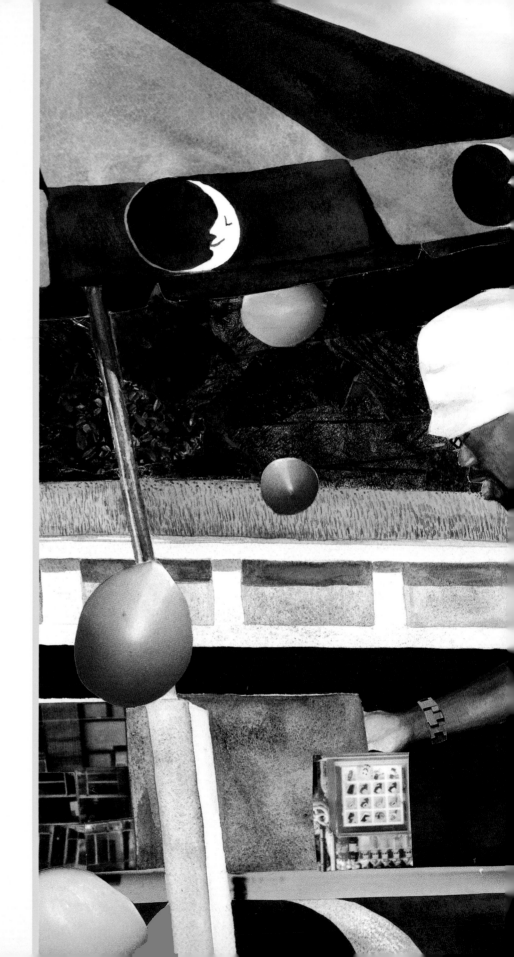

Welcome to the cool delight
of ice cream,
the sticky joy of peanut butter,
and the hint of honey
in chocolate fudge.

Welcome to the warm circle

of your daddy's arms,

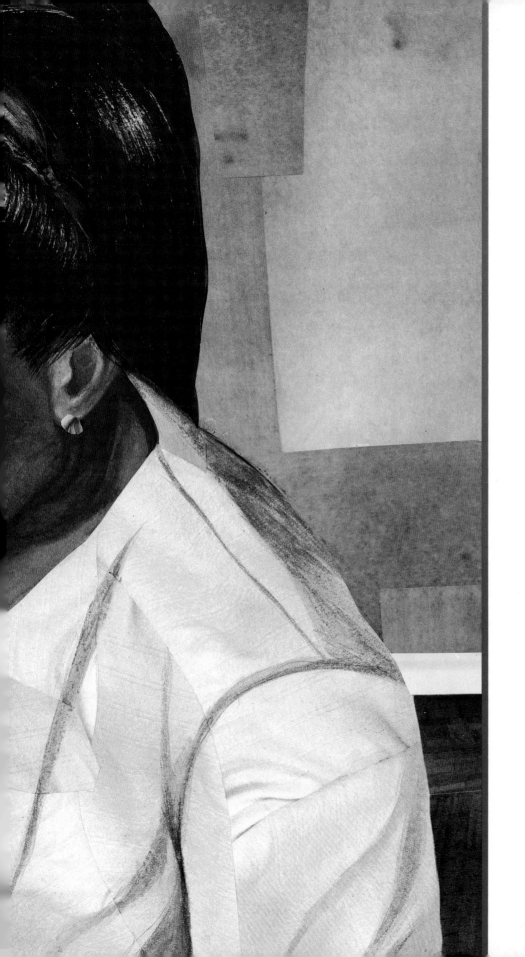

the slippery kisses

of your giddy grandmother,

and the cool tickle
of Mommy's nose
rubbing against your
belly button.

Welcome, Precious, to the squeaky surprise
of a yellow ducky
and the glistening mystery
of soap bubbles.

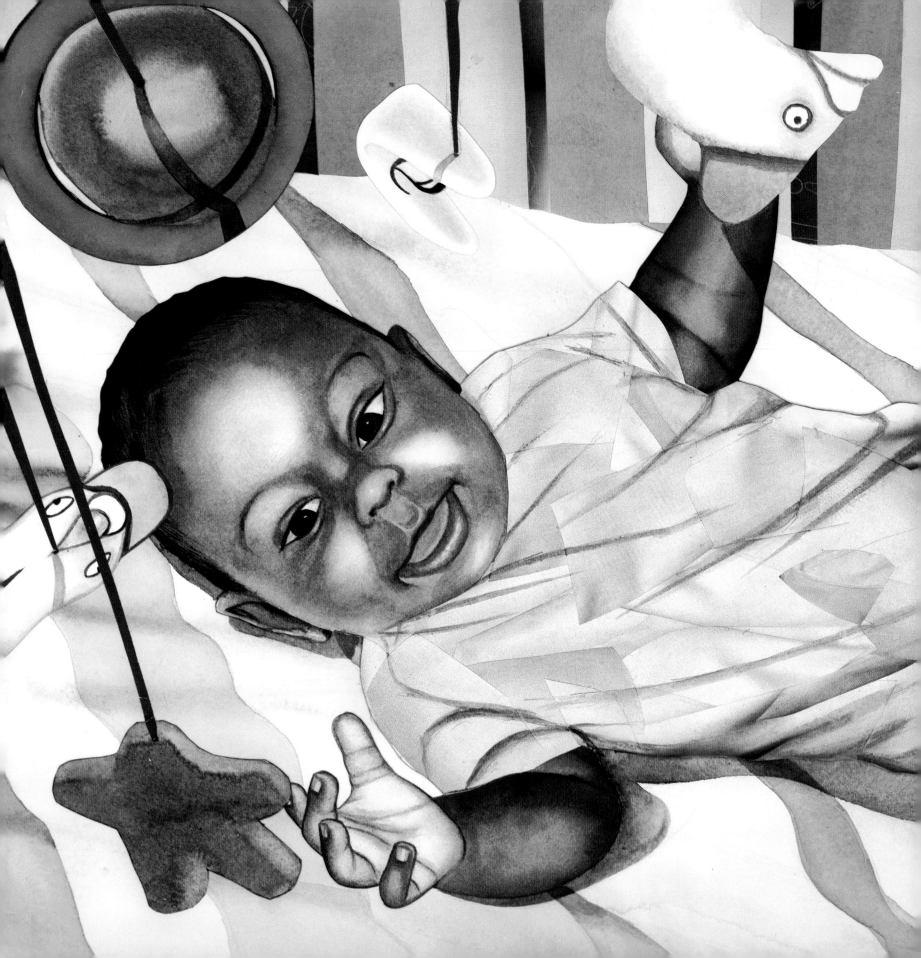

Oh, Precious,
life is a basket brimming
with things to see and hear,
taste and touch.

There is much
for you to learn!
But night crouches at the window,
and it is time for dreaming.

Lord willing, tomorrow will
soon knock
upon our door,
carrying her gift of hours.
Use them to explore.

For now, rest, Precious,
rest in the ark of my arms.
Rest, safe beneath the blanket
of love's lullaby.

For Elliot Mitchell Elisara

and every long-awaited little one.

—NG

Special thanks to Michael, Essie,

and their baby, Apre, for sharing their

time and life to make this project precious.

—BC

Text copyright © 2006 by Nikki Grimes

Illustrations copyright © 2006 by Bryan Collier

Library of Congress Cataloging-in-Publication Data

Grimes, Nikki.

Welcome, Precious / Nikki Grimes ; illustrations by Bryan Collier.-1st ed.   p. cm.

Summary: Illustrations and text welcome a new baby to some of life's delights, from "the glistening
mystery of soap bubbles" to "the swish of leaves in the breeze."

[1. Babies—Fiction.] I. Collier, Bryan, ill. II. Title.

PZ7.G88429Wel 2006   [E]–dc22   2005026996

ISBN 0-439-55702-X

10 9 8 7 6 5 4 3 2   06 07 08 09 10

Printed in Singapore   46

First edition, September 2006

The artwork was done in watercolor and collage.

Book design by Marijka Kostiw and Kristina Albertson